The Story of Levi's

by Michael Burgan • illustrated by Ron Himler

SCHOLASTIC INC.
New York Toronto London Auckland Sydney
Mexico City New Delhi Hong Kong Buenos Aires

Developed by Kirchoff/Wohlberg, Inc., in cooperation with Scholastic Inc.
Credits appear on the inside back cover, which constitutes an extension of this copyright page.
Copyright © 2002 by Scholastic Inc.
All rights reserved.   Published by Scholastic Inc.   Printed in the U.S.A.
ISBN 0-439-35181-2
SCHOLASTIC and associated logos and designs are trademarks
and/or registered trademarks of Scholastic Inc.
18   40   12 13/0

What kind of jeans do you like? Blue jeans are pants made of a cotton cloth called *denim*. Denim is flexible but also strong.

Sometimes blue jeans have diamonds on them. Some people cut their jeans off at the knee to make shorts. Some people wear blue jean overalls. Some people like to paint their blue jeans many colors. Some people even cut holes in the knees of their jeans! Some people fringe their jeans.

Would you like to know who made these pants so popular? His name is Levi Strauss, and this is his story.

Levi Strauss was born in 1829 in the southern German village of Buttenheim. At birth his first name was Loeb, but later he changed it to Levi. Strauss's father sold dry goods, such as cloth, clothes, needles, and scissors.

In the late 1830s, two of Levi Strauss's brothers, Jonas and Louis, had gone to America. They wanted to start their own business. In 1845, Levi Strauss's father died. Soon afterwards, Levi left Germany and joined his brothers in America.

Strauss arrived in New York in 1847. His brothers had started a business called J. Strauss Brother & Co. Like their father, the Strauss brothers sold dry goods. Levi Strauss learned this trade. Then he set out on his own.

For several years, Strauss sold dry goods in Kentucky. He was a peddler, or a traveling salesman.

After a few years, however, Strauss decided to move again. He had heard about the great California Gold Rush. Gold had been discovered in California in 1848. Thousands of miners raced there, hoping to strike it rich. Because many of them came in 1849, they were called forty-niners. Strauss did not want to mine gold. He thought he could make money another way.

He would sell dry goods to the miners and the other people flocking to California. He was taking his business to a place where he would have the most customers. Pretty smart, right? As you'll see, it was a smarter move than he could have predicted.

To make this move though, Strauss had to make a long trip. He made the voyage from New York to San Francisco in 1853. The typical trip to California was not easy. Strauss was traveling in the days before planes and trains, after all.

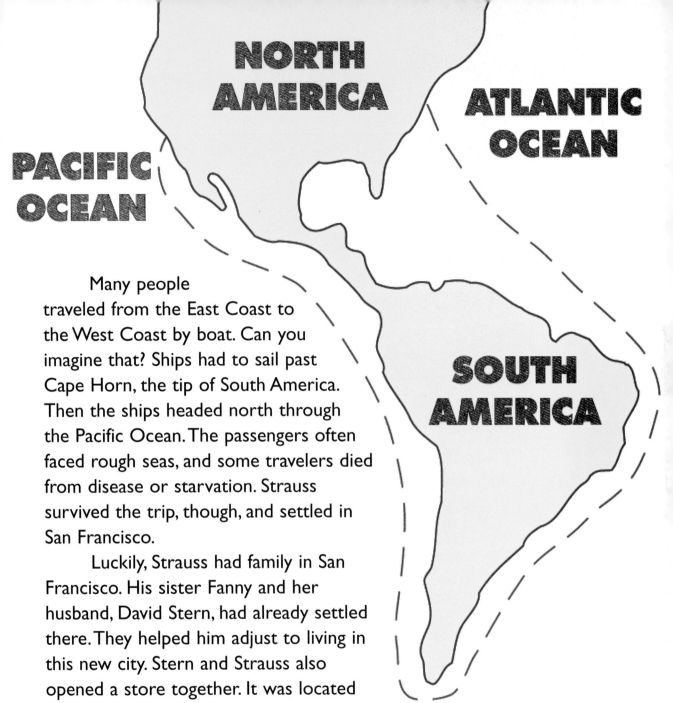

PACIFIC
OCEAN

NORTH
AMERICA

ATLANTIC
OCEAN

SOUTH
AMERICA

Many people traveled from the East Coast to the West Coast by boat. Can you imagine that? Ships had to sail past Cape Horn, the tip of South America. Then the ships headed north through the Pacific Ocean. The passengers often faced rough seas, and some travelers died from disease or starvation. Strauss survived the trip, though, and settled in San Francisco.

Luckily, Strauss had family in San Francisco. His sister Fanny and her husband, David Stern, had already settled there. They helped him adjust to living in this new city. Stern and Strauss also opened a store together. It was located near the city's docks and sold dry goods. Some of their store's items came from Strauss's brothers in New York. Other goods for sale included clothes for miners. The new business was called simply "Levi Strauss."

Strauss's company did well. San Francisco was still booming, thanks to the gold rush. Just a few years before, San Francisco had been a tiny trading post with less than a thousand citizens. Once the gold rush started, ship after ship arrived, full of people in search of gold. Many of them were called *prospectors*. The successful prospectors returned to San Francisco with nuggets of the yellow metal or bags filled with gold dust.

Often people who found gold decided to stay in San Francisco. By 1850, about 25,000 people had settled in the city. Before Strauss arrived, many newcomers lived in tents or wooden shacks. By the time Strauss arrived in San Francisco, the wealthy settlers were living in large, well-built homes.

The gold rush, however, did not last. Even as Strauss was starting his business, the miners were finding less gold. People kept coming to California, though. They also kept buying Strauss's dry goods. Strauss had customers outside of San Francisco, as well. At times, he took goods to small mining towns in the nearby mountains. Strauss sold supplies to the stores that served the miners' needs. The merchants who owned these stores trusted Strauss. They knew he sold quality items at a fair price.

Strauss's business continued to grow. He moved his store to bigger and better locations. In 1863, Strauss changed the store's name to Levi Strauss & Company. Three years later, the company moved again.

The new headquarters were fancier than the old ones. The building had fancy lights powered by gas. It also had a freight elevator. Very few buildings had elevators at that time. Strauss had clearly done very well for himself.

However, he would soon face a challenge.

California has long been famous for its earthquakes. San Francisco itself lies near a fault in the earth, where earthquakes often occur. Strauss had felt his first earthquake in 1865, but it had not done much damage. In 1868, however, a stronger earthquake shook the city.

The quake came in two waves. The second wave was the most deadly. As buildings shook, people ran out into the streets. Some buildings tumbled to the ground, killing people nearby. Several people died. No one in Strauss's family was hurt, but his company's building took a beating. A newspaper reported that the store was "cracked through and through."

Strauss had his workers move the goods out of the damaged building. Strauss then made repairs and soon reopened for business. He wouldn't let the earthquake put him out of business.

By now, Strauss was an important member of the community. He was involved with several charity groups. He also worked to help Europeans and Americans on the East Coast settle in California. In 1873, he would become a much more important member of the community.

One year before, in 1872, Strauss received a letter from Jacob Davis. Davis was a tailor in Reno, Nevada, who bought his cloth from Strauss. Davis knew Strauss was a successful and honest businessman. He needed Strauss's help with a new project.

There were many mines near Reno. Davis made work pants for miners. Sometimes he used a cotton material called duck cloth. Other times he used blue denim. One day a woman complained about her husband's work pants. She said they wore out or ripped too easily, especially near the pockets. As Davis made her husband's next pair of pants, he had an idea. He could use metal rivets to hold the cloth together at the pockets. The rivets would be much stronger than simple thread.

Davis's idea worked. Other miners saw the pants with rivets and wanted their own. Davis sold 200 pairs of these pants in little more than a year. Seeing how popular the pants were, Davis wanted to make more. He also wanted to make sure no one else would make riveted pants and take business away from him. He needed a patent. A patent is a legal document that keeps others from stealing an inventor's idea. Applying for a patent took money, though. Davis could not afford to take out a patent. That's why he turned to Levi Strauss.

Davis wanted Strauss to pay for the patent, which cost $68. The two men could then become partners. They would share the profits from the sale of the pants. Strauss quickly realized that the riveted pants were an excellent idea. He agreed to work with Davis to get the patent.

Getting a patent was not a simple task, however. To get a patent, an inventor must prove to the U.S. government that no one else has had a similar idea. At first, the government turned down Davis's request for a patent. Apparently, another company had used rivets in clothing made for soldiers during the Civil War. Finally, Davis and Strauss convinced the government that their idea was new and different. They received their patent on May 20, 1873.

Within weeks, Levi Strauss & Company sold its first pair of riveted pants. After one year, Strauss had sold more than 20,000 pants and coats with riveted pockets.

Levi Strauss & Company set up factories to produce its line of riveted clothes. Jacob Davis ran the factories. Inside the shops, a man called a *cutter* used a long knife to cut the thick cloth. Then women used sewing machines to assemble the pieces of cloth into pants.

Strauss's pants were a winning combination of good design and long-lasting material. Where did the denim he used come from? Well, the word *denim* is thought to come from the French words *de Nimes*. This means "from Nimes." The French city of Nimes was once a source for the strong blue cotton material.

Strauss, however, did not go to France for his cloth. A mill in New Hampshire had made denim since the Civil War. This mill provided the denim for Strauss's blue jeans. At the time, no one called the pants "blue jeans." Strauss called them "waist overalls."

People across the West bought Strauss's clothes. The company's ads sometimes showed cowboys wearing his waist overalls. People in Canada and several other countries sold his line of clothes. His company grew bigger and more famous.

Strauss put a special trademark on his pants, so everyone would know he made them. On the back pocket, workers sewed two lines with orange thread. The lines looked a little like the wings of a sea gull or the letter "V." Levi's jeans still have this trademark.

In the 1880s, Strauss added a label made of leather to the back of the pants. It showed two horses trying to pull apart a pair of his denim waist overalls. "It's no use," the label said. "They can't be ripped." The company promised to give customers a new pair if the pants ever ripped. Some people called Strauss's pants "the two-horse brand."

Thanks to his pants, Strauss became one of the richest men in San Francisco. He owned a hotel and other buildings in the city, along with his factories. He also bought his own wool mill. There he made wool to line some of his clothes. Wool-lined clothing kept people warm.

As Strauss got older, he was not as involved with his business. His nephews took care of the company's daily needs. Strauss became more involved with other companies. He sat on their boards of directors. This group of leaders makes long-range plans for a company. Strauss also continued to work with groups that helped the needy. He aided young people by donating money to pay for them to go to the University of California.

By 1902, Strauss's health was not always very good. On the night of September 26, he died in his sleep.

News of Strauss's death made the front page of the San Francisco newspapers. Hundreds of people came to his funeral. They included the rich men he had done business with and the workers from his factories. Some city businesses closed in Strauss's honor.

Although this great man was dead, his company had to go on. Strauss's nephews continued to run the business.

A few years later, disaster struck San Francisco. Another earthquake tore through the city. This one was much worse than the quake of 1868. All over the city, gas lines burst and started huge fires. The flames burned for days. When the fires finally ended, all of the Strauss company buildings were destroyed. Strauss's nephews did what they thought Levi would have done. They quickly began rebuilding the company.

Levi Strauss & Company grew strong again, though the famous blue denim pants went through some changes over the years. The original pants had buttons in the front. These buttons were replaced with a zipper. The company also added a new trademark. A small red tag was sewn on one of the back pockets. The tag had the company's name on it.

The pants also picked up new names. In 1942, the company officially called them "Levi's." Later, young people began to call them "jeans." This name came from a type of cloth once used to make workpants.

Whether they're called waist overalls, blue jeans, or Levi's, Strauss would be glad to know his pants have lasted so long.